Pets Are Fun

Chris George

PowerKiDS press
New York

Published in 2018 by The Rosen Publishing Group, Inc.
29 East 21st Street, New York, NY 10010

First Edition

Book Design: Ellina Litmanovich

Photo Credits: Cover, p. 1 Ermolaev Alexander/Shutterstock.com; p. 4 a katz/Shutterstock.com; p. 6 Susan Schmitz/Shutterstock.com; p. 8 Blend Images/Shutterstock.com; p. 10 Mbaldav/Thinkstock.com; p. 12 Jupiterimages/Thinkstock.com; p. 14 Stephen Denness/Shutterstock.com; p. 16 zeffirka84/Shutterstock.com; p. 18 Purestock/Thinkstock.com; p. 20 Susan Schmitz/Shutterstock.com; p. 22 Ermolaev Alexander/Shutterstock.com.

Cataloging-in-Publication Data
Names: George, Chris.
Title: Pets are fun / Chris George.
Description: New York : PowerKids Press, 2018. | Series: Early concepts | Includes index.
Identifiers: ISBN 9781508162216 (pbk.) | ISBN 9781508162230 (library bound) | ISBN 9781508162223 (6 pack) | ISBN 9781508162247 (ebook)
Subjects: LCSH: Pets–Juvenile literature.
Classification: LCC SF416.2 G46 2018 | DDC 636–dc23

CPSIA Compliance Information: Batch #BS17PK: For further information contact Rosen Publishing, New York, New York at 1-800-237-9932

Manufactured in the United States of America

CONTENTS

ADOPTABLE PETS

Finding a Pet

Pets are fun.
Where can you find a pet?
You can find pets in many places.
Let's go pick a pet!

Small Pets

Some pets are small.
Hamsters are small
and fun!
Hamsters are also
furry.
They sometimes
play with a ball.
Pet hamsters are
funny.

A fish is a small pet.
All fish live in water.
Fish swim all day long.
Look at this fish swim!

Is a pig a pet?
A guinea pig is a pet!
Guinea pigs eat pellets.
They like pumpkins, too.
They sometimes even chew shoes!

Did you know lizards
can be pets?
All lizards have scales.
And lizards lay eggs.
Some lizards eat
crickets.
All lizards need sun.
But lizards are fun!

Birds make good pets. Some birds sing songs. Those birds are noisy! This bird eats bird seed. This bird has blue feathers.

Rabbits are soft.
Rabbits love to hop!
This rabbit has big ears.
This rabbit eats lettuce.

Cats are great pets.
Cats take long naps.
Some cats love to cuddle.
Most cats like to nuzzle.
All cats love to play.

Dogs are cute pets.
Baby dogs are called
puppies.
Go ahead, rub this
puppy's tummy.
Puppies are truly
the best.

Picking a Pet

Big pet or small pet?
A pet that swims or
one that flies?
The pet with fur and
one that purrs?
So many pets
between them all!
Come on, let's pick
a pet.

Words to Know

guinea pig

hamster

lizard

Index